A Templar Book

Produced by The Templar Company plc,
Pippbrook Mill, London Road, Dorking, Surrey RH4 1JE, Great Britain.

This edition produced for Parragon Books,
Unit 13-17, Avonbridge Trading Estate, Atlantic Road, Avonmouth, Bristol BS11 9QD

This book contains material first published as
The Wonderful Scooter in Let's Read
First published by Birn Bros. 1933

Illustrated by Angela Mills

Printed and bound in Italy

ISBN 1 85813 652 0

Enid Blyton's

POCKET LIBRARY

THE MAGIC BICYCLE

Illustrated by Angela Mills

·PARRAGON·

Peter had a lovely new bicycle for his birthday. It was painted bright red with a yellow seat, and on the handle bars was a bright silver bell.

It was a fine bell, and had a very loud ring. You should have seen everybody jump when Peter cycled up and rang it just behind them.

Peter went out on his bicycle every day after school, just before tea. It was great fun cycling up and down the lane, ring-ringing all the way.

But one afternoon a strange thing happened to Peter. He was cycling along whistling happily to himself, watching rabbits scamper along the grassy verge.

When he came to the little hill that ran down to the sweet-shop at the bottom, he took both his feet off the pedals and had a lovely ride – but, do you know, when he reached the bottom of the hill the bicycle wouldn't stop.

No, it went on, all by itself without Peter doing anything to help it. He was so surprised.

"What a funny thing!" he thought. "What's happened to my bicycle, why is it going by itself? Ooh! It's going faster! My goodness, I hope we don't run into anyone."

On and on went the little red bicycle, with Peter holding on tightly. It went faster and faster, and Peter had to hold on tightly to his cap, in case it blew away.

The bicycle raced through the village and made everyone jump quickly out of the way. It nearly knocked over Mister Plod, the policeman. Poor Peter couldn't possibly say he was sorry because the bicycle didn't stop.

On and on it went, up hills and down hills, along the country lanes, past fields and farmyards. At last the little red bicycle ran into a village Peter had never seen before. It was a strange place. The houses all looked like dolls' houses, and there was a farm exactly like Peter's toy farm in the nursery at home with funny wooden-looking trees standing in rows, and wooden-looking cows grazing in the fields.

And what do think were in the
street? – why, toys, all standing
about and talking to one another,
or shopping busily.

"This must be Toy Town," said
Peter to himself, in great surprise.
"Perhaps my bicycle came from
here and felt homesick suddenly,
and raced back home."

In the middle of the street was a wooden policeman, holding up his hand to stop the traffic. The bicycle tried to get past – but the policeman grabbed the handlebars and stopped it. Off fell Peter, landing with a bump.

"Why didn't you stop?" cried the policeman, crossly. "Didn't you see my hand put out?"

"Yes, but my bicycle wouldn't stop," said Peter. "It won't do what I tell it to!"

"I don't believe a word of it," said the policeman, getting out his notebook. "Show me your bicycle licence, please."

"But I haven't got one," said Peter, in surprise. "You don't need to have a bicycle licence where I come from – you only have licences for motor cars and television sets."

"In Toy Town you have to have a licence for bicycles too," said the policeman, sharply.

"You must come to the police-station with me, and pay a fine."
"But I haven't any money," said Peter, quite frightened.

ENID BLYTON'S POCKET LIBRARY·

"Never mind," said the policeman. "You can pay your fine in chocolate money instead."

"I don't have any chocolate money either," wailed Peter. But it made no difference. The policeman took him by the arm, and marched him down the street. Suddenly there came a great noise of shouting not far off, and a big brown teddy bear rushed by, carrying a little bottle of brightly coloured sweets.

"Stop thief, stop thief!" cried a little wooden shopkeeper dressed in a stripy apron. And all the toys standing around in the street began to chase the teddy bear, but he jumped into a toy motor car and whizzed off at top speed.

Two more toy policemen rushed up. "Who has another motor car that we can use to chase him?" they cried. But nobody had. Then Peter had a fine idea.

"I'll go after him on my bicycle!" he said. "Jump up behind me, policemen, and I'll scoot after that naughty teddy."

In a trice he was back on his bicycle, and behind him crowded the three wooden policemen, and another teddy bear who wanted to join in the fun.

Peter pedalled as fast as he could, and soon he could see the teddy bear up ahead of him in the toy motor car.

The teddy looked behind him
and saw that he was being chased.
He went faster still, but Peter
pedalled as hard as he could and
soon he had nearly caught up.

Suddenly the clockwork motor car the teddy was driving began to run down. It went slower and slower, until finally it stopped. The teddy got out to wind it up again – but before he had given it more than one wind, Peter had pedalled alongside.

The policemen jumped off and grabbed the naughty teddy. They made him give up the bottle of sweets and said he must clean the whole sweet shop from top to bottom to show that he was sorry.

"Well," said the wooden policeman who had stopped Peter when he first arrived in the little village, "that was a very good idea of yours, to let us chase that teddy on your bicycle."

"That's quite all right," said Peter. "I was glad to help."

"Thanks very much anyway," said the policeman. "I won't say any more about your not having a bicycle licence. You can go home now – but please be sure to have a licence if you come to Toy Town again."

"Thank you," said Peter, sitting down on the grassy roadside. He was very hot and tired after his long cycle ride.

"It's been a great adventure. But I do wish I didn't have to cycle all the way home again. This bicycle of mine won't seem to go by itself any more, and I shall have to pedal it up all of those hills."

"Dear me, I didn't think about your being tired," said the policeman, very much upset. "Look here – get into this car with me – the one the teddy used. You can put your bicycle in the back. Can you drive a car?"

"No," said Peter, "not even a toy one, I'm afraid."

"What a nuisance," said the policeman. "I can't drive either." Then the clever policeman had a wonderful idea.

"Hey, Teddy Bear!" he cried to the miserable bear who was still being marched off down the road. "You can drive this car, can't you? You can do something else useful to make up for all the trouble you've caused."

"Oh! Yes," said the bear, pleased to show how clever he was. "Jump in everyone, and I'll drive Peter all the way home, if he will tell me where he lives."

Off they all went, right through Toy Town and back to the village where Peter lived. How his friends stared when they saw him drive up with three wooden policemen and two teddy bears – but before they could ask them any questions the

toys had driven off again, and Peter was left standing by his gate with his little red bicycle.

"What an adventure," he said. And it certainly was, wasn't it?